ADINE'S IGLOO

Level 6C

Written by Lucy George
Illustrated by Monica Armino

What is synthetic phonics?

Synthetic phonics teaches children to recognise the sounds of letters and to blend (synthesise) them together to make whole words.

Understanding sound/letter relationships gives children the confidence and ability to read unfamiliar words, without having to rely on memory or guesswork; this helps them to progress towards independent reading.

Did you know? Spoken English uses more than 40 speech sounds. Each sound is called a *phoneme*. Some phonemes relate to a single letter (d–o–g) and others to combinations of letters (sh–ar–p). When a phoneme is written down it is called a *grapheme*. Teaching these sounds, matching them to their written form and sounding out words for reading is the basis of synthetic phonics.

Consultant

I love reading phonics has been created in consultation with language expert Abigail Steel. She has a background in teaching and teacher training and is a respected expert in the field of synthetic phonics. Abigail Steel is a regular contributor to educational publications. Her international education consultancy supports parents and teachers in the promotion of literacy skills.

Reading tips

This book focuses on two sounds made with the letter i: i as in fin and igh as in find.

Tricky words in this book

Any words in bold may have unusual spellings or are new and have not yet been introduced.

> Tricky word in this book:
>
> ## whistle

Extra ways to have fun with this book

After the reader has read the story, ask them questions about what they have just read:

Where in the world does Adine live?
What does Adine do with her father?

I love it when Adine reads a story to me in our igloo!

A pronunciation guide

This grid contains the sounds used in the stories in levels 4, 5 and 6 and a guide on how to say them. /a/ represents the sounds made, rather than the letters in a word.

/ai/ as in game	/ai/ as in play/they	/ee/ as in leaf/these	/ee/ as in he
/igh/ as in kite/light	/igh/ as in find/sky	/oa/ as in home	/oa/ as in snow
/oa/ as in cold	/y+oo/ as in cube/music/new	long /oo/ as in flute/crew/blue	/oi/ as in boy
/er/ as in bird/hurt	/or/ as in snore/oar/door	/or/ as in dawn/sauce/walk	/e/ as in head
/e/ as in said/any	/ou/ as in cow	/u/ as in touch	/air/ as in hare/bear/there
/eer/ as in deer/here/cashier	/t/ as in tripped/skipped	/d/ as in rained	/j/ as in gent/gin/gym
/j/ as in barge/hedge	/s/ as in cent/circus/cyst	/s/ as in prince	/s/ as in house
/ch/ as in itch/catch	/w/ as in white	/h/ as in who	/r/ as in write/rhino

Sounds this story focuses on are highlighted in the grid.

/**f**/ as in phone	/**f**/ as in rough	/**ul**/ as in pencil/ hospital	/**z**/ as in fries/ cheese/breeze
/**n**/ as in knot/ gnome/engine	/**m**/ as in welcome /thumb/column	/**g**/ as in guitar/ghost	/**zh**/ as in vision/beige
/**k**/ as in chord	/**k**/ as in plaque/ bouquet	/**nk**/ as in uncle	/**ks**/ as in box/books/ ducks/cakes
/**a**/ and /**o**/ as in hat/what	/**e**/ and /**ee**/ as in bed/he	/**i**/ and /**igh**/ as in fin/find	/**o**/ and /**oa**/ as in hot/cold
/**u**/ and short /**oo**/ as in but/put	/**ee**/, /**e**/ and /**ai**/ as in eat/ bread/break	/**igh**/, /**ee**/ and /**e**/ as in tie/field/friend	/**ou**/ and /**oa**/ as in cow/blow
/**ou**/, /**oa**/ and /**oo**/ as in out/ shoulder/could	/**i**/ and /**ai**/ as in money/they	/**c**/ and /**s**/ as in cat/cent	/**y**/, /**igh**/ and /**i**/ as in yes/sky/myth
/**g**/ and /**j**/ as in got/giant	/**ch**/, /**c**/ and /**sh**/ as in chin/ school/chef	/**er**/, /**air**/ and /**eer**/ as in earth/bear/ears	/**u**/, /**ou**/ and /**oa**/ as in plough/dough

Be careful not to add an 'uh' sound to 's', 't', 'p', 'c', 'h', 'r', 'm', 'd', 'g', 'l', 'f' and 'b'. For example, say 'fff' not 'fuh' and 'sss' not 'suh'.

Far in the north, near the Arctic Circle, cold winds blow. Piles of snow lie thick on the ground and line the hills.

In this chilly land lives Adine,
with her family. They are known
as Inuit.

On hunting days Adine goes
with her father to find food.

They drill a hole in the ice
and unwind the line
to catch fish for dinner.

On wild days she stays behind
with her mother.

They sit inside the igloo
and stitch with fine needles,
making clothes from animal hides.

On clear days she plays with her friends.

They climb up the piles of snow and hike up the hill...

...then they glide back to the igloo!

At dinner time, Adine finds
kindling for a fire.

When the fire is lit, they bring food from hunting.

The family sit around the fire,
and cook the fish. Sometimes
they sing in the dim light.

When the sky grows dark, they watch the lights in the sky, called the aurora borealis.

Sometimes the children **whistle**
to blow away bad spirits.

At bedtime, Adine climbs into her igloo and she lies on thick animal skins.

She makes a wish before she blows
out the light and falls asleep. She
is warm and cosy, tucked up tightly
in her favourite place: her igloo.

OVER **48** TITLES IN SIX LEVELS
Abigail Steel recommends...

Some titles from Level 4

I love reading phonics — **The Maze**
978-1-84898-559-9

I love reading phonics — **Fairy Fay's Bad Day**
978-1-84898-560-5

I love reading phonics — **Pirate School**
978-1-84898-566-7

Some titles from Level 5

I love reading phonics — **Snapped by Sam**
978-1-84898-561-2

I love reading phonics — **Max's Trip**
978-1-84898-562-9

I love reading phonics — **George the Genius Gerbil**
978-1-84898-567-4

Other titles to enjoy from Level 6

I love reading phonics — **What Wally Wanted**
978-1-84898-563-6

I love reading phonics — **Superhero Ed**
978-1-84898-564-3

I love reading phonics — **The Robot Bop**
978-1-84898-570-4

An Hachette UK Company
www.hachette.co.uk

Copyright © Octopus Publishing Group Ltd 2012
First published in Great Britain in 2012 by TickTock, an imprint of Octopus Publishing Group Ltd,
Endeavour House, 189 Shaftesbury Avenue, London WC2H 8JY.
www.octopusbooks.co.uk

ISBN 978 1 84898 569 8

Printed and bound in China
10 9 8 7 6 5 4 3 2 1